Dear Parent:
Your child's love of reading starts here!

Every child learns to read in a different way and at his or her own speed. Some go back and forth between reading levels and read favorite books again and again. Others read through each level in order. You can help your young reader improve and become more confident by encouraging his or her own interests and abilities. From books your child reads with you to the first books he or she reads alone, there are I Can Read Books for every stage of reading:

SHARED READING
Basic language, word repetition, and whimsical illustrations, ideal for sharing with your emergent reader

BEGINNING READING
Short sentences, familiar words, and simple concepts for children eager to read on their own

READING WITH HELP
Engaging stories, longer sentences, and language play for developing readers

READING ALONE
Complex plots, challenging vocabulary, and high-interest topics for the independent reader

ADVANCED READING
Short paragraphs, chapters, and exciting themes for the perfect bridge to chapter books

I Can Read Books have introduced children to the joy of reading since 1957. Featuring award-winning authors and illustrators and a fabulous cast of beloved characters, I Can Read Books set the standard for beginning readers.

A lifetime of discovery begins with the magical words "I Can Read!"

Visit www.icanread.com for information
on enriching your child's reading experience.

The Dark Knight: Batman's Friends and Foes
BATMAN and all related characters and elements are trademarks of DC Comics © 2008.
All Rights Reserved.
Printed in the United States of America.
No part of this book may be used or reproduced in any manner whatsoever without written permission
except in the case of brief quotations embodied in critical articles and reviews.
For information address HarperCollins Children's Books, a division of HarperCollins Publishers,
1350 Avenue of the Americas, New York, NY 10019.
www.icanread.com

Library of Congress catalog number: 2008922483
ISBN 978-0-06-156190-0
Cover art by Cameron Stewart and Dave McCaig
Book design by John Sazaklis
❖
First Edition

I Can Read!

READING
2
WITH HELP

THE DARK KNIGHT™

BATMAN'S FRIENDS AND FOES

ADAPTED BY **CATHERINE HAPKA**
PENCILS BY **ADRIAN BARRIOS**
DIGITAL PAINTS BY **KANILA TRIPP**

INSPIRED BY THE FILM **THE DARK KNIGHT**
SCREENPLAY BY
JONATHAN NOLAN AND **CHRISTOPHER NOLAN**
STORY BY **CHRISTOPHER NOLAN** & **DAVID S. GOYER**
BATMAN CREATED BY **BOB KANE**

HarperCollins*Publishers*

Gotham City can be
a dark and scary place.
The people who live there
need a hero to protect them.
That hero is Batman.
He leads the fight against evil.

Only a few people know
Batman's true identity.
By day he is Bruce Wayne,
a rich businessman.

But when there is trouble,

the Bat-Signal lights up the sky.

Then Bruce becomes Batman

and swoops to the rescue.

Batman has a lot to do
to clean up Gotham City.
It is full of bad guys
like the Chechen.

The Chechen is a thug from Russia.

He loves his three mean dogs.

But he doesn't like Batman!

The Scarecrow is an old foe.

He has fought Batman before.

But he is still up to no good.

These days Batman

has even more bad guys

to worry about.

One day a gang of clowns robs a bank.

They break into the safe

and steal all the money.

But one of the clowns

betrays the others.

He gets away with all the cash!

That clown is really the Joker.
He is a crazy criminal
with big scars on his face.

The Joker always
appears to be smiling.
But he is serious about
causing trouble for Gotham City.

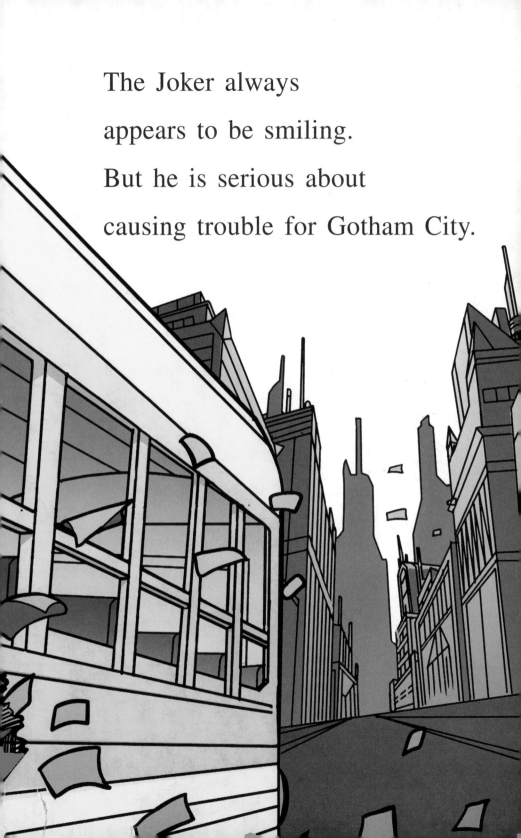

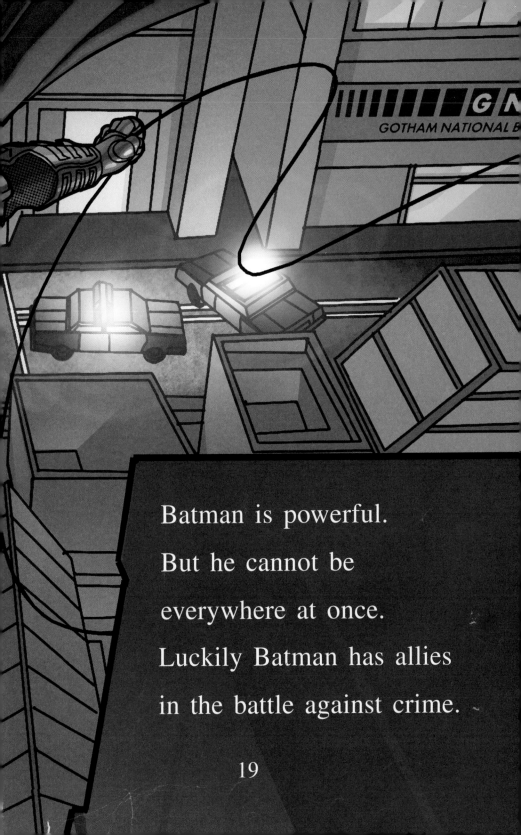

Batman is powerful.
But he cannot be
everywhere at once.
Luckily Batman has allies
in the battle against crime.

Alfred is Bruce Wayne's
trusted butler.

He is also his oldest friend.

Alfred is one of the few people
who knows that Bruce is Batman,
but he is very loyal.
He would never give away
the secret.

Rachel Dawes is another old friend.

She knows the truth about Batman, too.

Rachel has an important job
in the city government.
She helps any way she can.

Police Lieutenant Gordon
runs the Gotham Police Department.
He turns on the Bat-Signal
whenever there is trouble.

"I like to remind everyone that Batman is out there," he says.

Lucius Fox helps Bruce Wayne
run Wayne Enterprises.
He is very smart and creative.

Lucius also helps Bruce a lot
by creating the tools and weapons
he needs to become Batman.

Harvey Dent is Rachel's new boss.

He is tough on crime.

He works with the law
to put criminals behind bars.

"I will stop the crime wave
in this city," Harvey tells Rachel.
He doesn't know Batman's identity.
But he knows the masked stranger
wants to clean up Gotham, too.

25¢

The Gotham Times

BATMAN CLEANS UP
CRIME IN GOTHAM

Yes, Gotham City can be
a dark and scary place.
The Joker and the other bad guys
make sure of that.

But Batman's friends and allies help to make him even stronger.

With his friends at his side,

Batman will triumph

and restore peace to Gotham City!